Books inspired by the television series

Bibliothèque et Archives nationales du Québec and
Library and Archives Canada cataloguing in publication

Jolin, Dominique, 1964-
[Camping de nuit. English]
Camp Out
(Toopy and Binoo)
Translation of: Camping de nuit.
For children.

ISBN 978-1-55389-044-7

I. Tremblay, Carole, 1959- . II. Simon, Karen.
III. Title. IV. Title: Camping de nuit. English.
V. Series: Jolin, Dominique, 1964- . Toopy and Binoo.
PS8569.O399C3513 2009 jC843'.54 C2009-940331-5
PS9569.O399C3513 2009

This text is adapted from an episode of the television series *Toopy and Binoo* produced by Spectra Animation Inc., with the participation of Treehouse.
Original script by Gerard Lewis
Writing director: Katherine Sandford

We would like to thank Télé-Québec and
Treehouse for their collaboration.

Collection director: Carole Tremblay
Editor: Jacqueline Snider
Artistic and graphic direction and *Toopy and Binoo* typeface design by Primeau Barey

Legal Deposit: 3rd Quarter 2009
Bibliothèque et Archives nationales du Québec
National Library of Canada

Dominique et compagnie
300 Arran Street, Saint-Lambert, Quebec, Canada J4R 1K5
Tel.: 514 875-0327 Fax: 450 672-5448
E-mail: dominiqueetcie@editionsheritage.com

www.dominiqueetcompagnie.com

Printed in China

We acknowledge the support of the Canada Council for the Arts for our publishing program.

We acknowledge the financial support of the Government of Canada through the Book Publishing Industry Development Program (BPIDP) for our publishing activities.

Government of Québec – Publishing Program and Tax Credit Program – Gestion SODEC.

Camp Out

Text by Dominique Jolin and Carole Tremblay
English Text by Karen Simon
From the original script by Gerard Lewis
Illustrations taken from the television series *Toopy and Binoo*

SPECTRA ANIMATION
Dominique & Friends

"Binoo, want to go camping?"
asks Toopy.
"Come on, say yes. Please, please, please!"
Binoo agrees.
"Fantastic!" exclaims Toopy.
"Come and see! I've already set up the tent."

Binoo crawls into the tent while Toopy
runs to turn out the light.
"I just love camping!" says Toopy when he returns.
"There's nothing like it in the whole world!"
But there's not much light inside the tent,
and Binoo is a bit uneasy.
"Hmmm... maybe it's a little too dark,"
says Toopy. "Come Binoo, let's go find a night light."

The two friends leave the tent.
"It's dark here too," says Toopy. "Hey, I have an idea!"
Toopy switches on his helmet light.
"Okaaay! Now we can see where we're going. Follow me, Binoo!"

But before they get very far they hear a noise in the bushes. Slowly Toopy walks toward the noise and discovers... a racoon fast asleep!
"Um... good evening, Mr. Racoon. Do you know where we can find a night light?"
Mr. Racoon doesn't answer. He'd rather look for a quieter place to sleep.

A bit further along, Toopy and Binoo meet a squirrel.
"Um... good evening, Mr. Squirrel," says Toopy.
Mr. Squirrel seems very nervous. He squeaks and squeaks.
"Is something wrong, Mr. Squirrel?" asks Toopy.
"What? I'm standing on your *what*? Oh, your tail! I'm so sorry!"
Toopy moves his foot and the squirrel runs away.
"Wait a minute! Stay! I love squirrels."

Suddenly, Toopy hears a strange “Whoo hoo” sound.
“Did you hear that, Binoo?”
The two friends look up and discover... an owl!
Toopy’s light woke the owl up.
Before Toopy can talk to him, Mr. Owl rubs his
eyes and goes back into his house.
“Ohhh... he’s sooo cute,” says Toopy.
“I just love owls!”

Next Toopy and Binoo find a swamp. A colony of frogs are building a house of cards on a lily pad. “Good evening, Frogs,” says Toopy. “Do you know where we can find a night light?”
Oh no! The house of cards falls down and the frogs are angry. Toopy can’t understand what they’re saying. He thinks they’re giving him directions.
“Uh... over there? Are you sure? Thank you. Did you understand any of that, Binoo?”

A bit further along in the
forest Toopy and Binoo see
Mrs. Bear. She's just put
her little ones to bed.
"Good evening, Mrs. Bear,"
says Toopy. "We're looking
for a night light..."
Then Toopy sees the baby
bears fast asleep.
"Oh, little baby bears!
They're so funny!"

Uh-oh! The baby bears have woken up!
Mrs. Bear is not at all pleased.
“Shhh!” she says.
“Oh, I’m so sorry,” says Toopy.
Toopy and Binoo leave. They still haven’t
found a night light.

"Don't worry, Binoo," says Toopy.
"We'll find one somewhere."
Binoo points to Toopy's helmet and smiles.
"What is it, Binoo? Have you found something?
A light? Where? Where is it?"
Toopy takes off his helmet and looks at it. Surprise!
"A NIGHT LIGHT!!! We've found a night light!
It's perfect, Binoo! I knew we'd find one!
Now, we just have to find the tent."

"Oh tent, where are you?"
Binoo shows Toopy the tent.
"Aha! You found it! Bravo, Binoo! Now we can camp out!"
The two friends get comfortable inside the tent.

"Binoo, you really are the best," says Toopy.
"First you found a night light. Then you found the tent.
You always find everything you look for.
Who knows what great things you'll find tomorrow."

“Shhh!”